Dreamtivity

# SPOT THE DIFFERENCE
## Which puppy is different?

Your answer:

Answer: B

# CIRCLE THE TWO THAT MATCH.

Your answers:

☐ & ☐

# WHICH THREE PIECES COMPLETE THE PICTURE?

Your answers:

# SPOT THE DIFFERENCE
## Which puppy is different?

Your answer:

# HOW MANY WORDS CAN YOU MAKE USING THE LETTERS IN:

## PUPPY DOG CUDDLES

_____

_____

_____

_____

_____

_____

_____

# UNSCRAMBLE THE LETTERS TO REVEAL THE WORD.

T A R B B I

_ _ _ _ _ _

Y U P P P

_ _ _ _ _

R E L Q U S I R

_ _ _ _ _ _ _ _

T N I T E K

_ _ _ _ _ _

R E D E

_ _ _ _

# HELP FIND THE BALLS.

# HOW MANY TIMES CAN YOU FIND THE WORD:
## CUTE

U E T U C
C E C U E
C U T E T
U E T U U
C U T E C

Your answer:

# WHICH THREE PIECES COMPLETE THE PICTURE?

Your answers:

# HELP THE PUPPY FIND HIS TOYS.

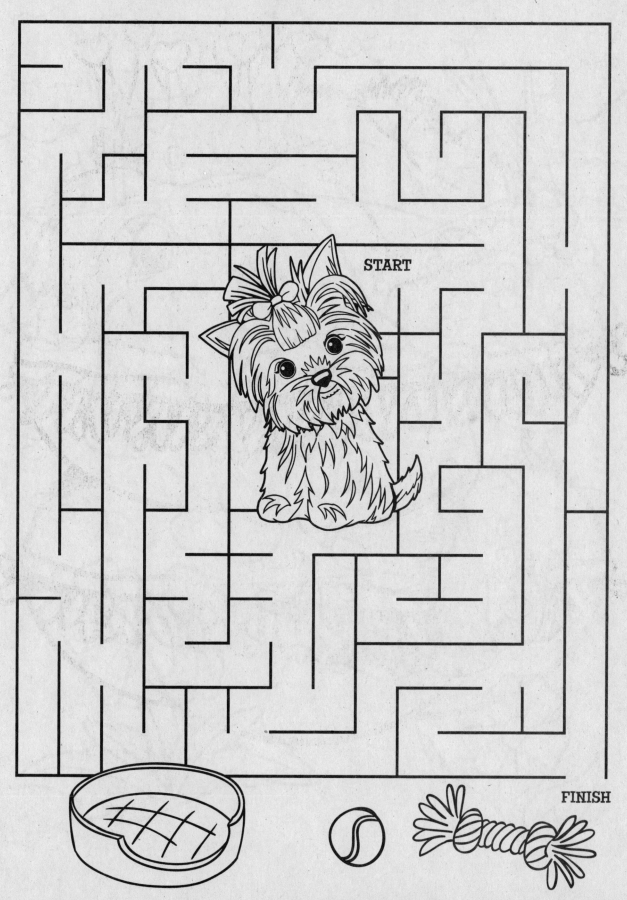

START

FINISH

# PUZZLED?
## Which piece completes the picture?

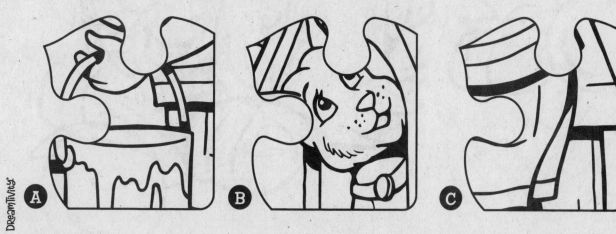

A B C

# CONNECT THE DOTS.

# WHICH LINE LEADS THE PUPPY TO HER PLAYMATE?

A

B

C

D

Your answer:

Answer: C

# HELP THE PUPPY FIND HIS HOUSE.

START

FINISH

FIDO

# PUZZLED?
## Which piece completes the picture?

A

B

C

# WHAT IS THE DIFFERENCE?

Circle 5 differences between this picture
and the one on the opposite page.

# HEY, KIDS!
## WE WANT TO SEE YOUR CREATIVITY!

# Be part of TeamTivity™

We love seeing your work! Color or complete a favorite page from any Dreamtivity book. Have a grown-up photograph or scan it, and share your masterpiece with the team. It's that easy! You never know, we might display it for all to see!

## NOW, GO COLOR YOUR WORLD!

Upload your art to: facebook.com/dreamtivity
Or email it to: teamtivity@dreamtivity.net
*Be sure to include your child's first name and age.*
*Tell us your favorite thing to color.*

**\*TeamTivity is our fun connection with creative kids everywhere! We aim to inspire, encourage and champion their creativity!**

TeamTivity™
CREATIVE KID!

YOUR NAME _____
I sent my masterpiece on _____
and now I am a part of the team!         DATE
DReamTivity®   NOW, GO COLOR YOUR WORLD!

Cut along dashed line and keep for yourself.